The Three Bears

The Little Red Hen

The Three Little Pigs

The Three Bears

Papa Bear, Mama Bear
and Baby Bear lived in a
cottage in the woods.

One day, Mama Bear made porridge.
It was too hot to eat, so the bears
went for a walk to let it cool.
While they were out, a little girl
named Goldilocks came to the door.
She smelled the porridge and
went inside.

Goldilocks took a taste
from Papa Bear's big bowl.
It was much too hot.

She took a taste from
Mama Bear's bowl.
It was much too cold.

She took a taste from Baby Bear's bowl,

and it was just right. So she ate it all up!

Goldilocks sat in Papa Bear's chair. It was too hard.

She sat in Mama Bear's chair. It was too soft.

She sat in Baby Bear's chair. It was just right

until the seat broke and Goldilocks fell down!

Goldilocks was sleepy, so she went upstairs.

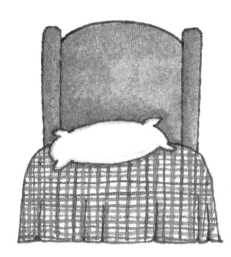

Papa Bear's pillow
was too big.

Mama Bear's pillow
was too flat.

Baby Bear's pillow was just right. Goldilocks
crawled in, pulled up the covers
and fell fast asleep.
She didn't even wake up
when the three bears came
home for breakfast.

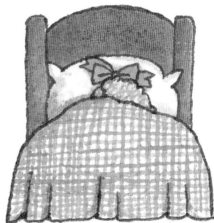

"Somebody's been eating my porridge!"
Papa Bear roared.

"Somebody's been eating my porridge!"
Mama Bear cried.

"Somebody's been eating my porridge," squeaked
Baby Bear. "And they have eaten it all up!"

"Somebody's been sitting in my chair!" Papa Bear roared.

"Somebody's been sitting in my chair!"
Mama Bear cried.

"Somebody's been sitting in my chair,
and it is all broken," squeaked Baby Bear.

The three bears went upstairs.
"Somebody's been sleeping
in my bed!" Papa Bear roared.

"Somebody's been
sleeping in my bed!"
Mama Bear cried.

"Somebody's been sleeping in my bed,"

squeaked Baby Bear. "And she's still here!"

Goldilocks woke up and saw the three bears.
"Oh, my," she said,
and ran all the way home.

And the three bears never

saw Goldilocks

again.

The Little Red Hen

One day, the little red hen found
a grain of wheat in the farmyard.
"Who will help me plant it?" she asked.
   "Not I," said the duck. "Not I," said the cat.
      "Not I," said the dog.
         "I will plant it myself," she said
Soon the wheat was tall and ripe.

"Who will help me cut the wheat?" she asked.

"Not I," said the duck. "Not I," said the cat.

"Not I," said the dog.

"I will cut it myself," she said.

"Who will help me thresh it?" she asked.

"Not I," said the duck. "Not I," said the cat.

"Not I," said the dog.

"I will thresh it myself," she said.

"Who will help me turn the wheat into flour?" she asked.

"Not I," said the duck. "Not I," said the cat.

"Not I," said the dog.

"I will do it myself," she said.

"Who will help me make the bread?" she asked.

"Not I," said the duck. "Not I," said the cat.

"Not I," said the dog.

"Then I will make it myself," she said.

The little red hen baked a lovely loaf of bread.

"I will help you eat it!" said the duck.

"I will help you eat it!" said the cat.

"I will help you eat it!" said the dog.

"Oh, no, you won't," said the little red hen.

"I and my chicks will eat the bread."

The Three
Little Pigs

Once upon a time, a mother pig lived
in a house with her three little pigs.
One day, the little pigs decided to go
and live on their own.
So the mother pig waved them
good-bye, and off they went.

The first little pig wanted to build a house made of straw. He had just finished it when along came a wolf.

"Little pig, let me come in!" he called.

"No," said the little pig.

"Not by the hair of my chinny-chin-chin."

"Then I'll huff and I'll puff and I'll blow your house in!" shouted the wolf.

He huffed and he puffed,

and he blew the house in.

The second little pig wanted to build a house made of sticks. He had just finished it when along came the wolf.

"Little pig, let me come in!" he called.

"No," said the little pig.

"Not by the hair of my chinny-chin-chin."

"Then I'll huff and I'll puff and I'll blow your house in!" shouted the wolf.

He huffed and he puffed,
and he blew the house in.

The third little pig wanted to build a house made of bricks. He had just finished it when along came the wolf.

"Little pig, let me come in!" he called.

"No," said the little pig.

"Not by the hair of my chinny-chin-chin."

"Then I'll huff and I'll puff and I'll blow your house in!" shouted the wolf.

He huffed and he puffed,
but he couldn't blow in
the little brick house.

"Little pig, I'm going to climb down the chimney!"
But the little pig had a hot fire in the fireplace below.
So the wolf had to give up and go away.